Just Because You're Mine

Just Because You're Mine

By Sally Lloyd-Jones

Illustrated by Frank Endersby

HARPER

An Imprint of HarperCollinsPublishers

Just Because You're Mine
Text copyright © 2012 by Sally Lloyd-Jones
Illustrations copyright © 2012 by Frank Endersby

Library of Congress Cataloging-in-Publication Data
Lloyd-Jones, Sally.
    Just because you're mine / by Sally Lloyd-Jones ; illustrated by Frank Endersby. – 1st ed.
       p.   cm.
    Summary: Little Red Squirrel spends a day showing his father all of the wonderful things he can
do, as he tries to guess why Daddy loves him.
    ISBN 978-0-06-201476-4 (trade bdg.) – ISBN 978-0-06-201477-1 (lib. bdg.)
    [1. Fathers and sons–Fiction.   2. Love–Fiction.   3. Red squirrels–Fiction.   4. Squirrels–
Fiction.]   I. Endersby, Frank, ill.   II. Title.   III. Title: Just because you are mine.
PZ7.L77878Jus 2012   2010018439
[E]–dc22

Typography by Jeanne L. Hogle
12 13 14 15 16 LPR 10 9 8 7 6 5 4 3 2
❖
First Edition

For John-Mark, with love

—S.L.-J.

For Lilly

—F.E.

Little Red Squirrel and his daddy were
playing in the big wood.

"Daddy!" shouted Little Red Squirrel. "Look at me!"
And he scampered off.

First Little Red Squirrel showed his dad his Super Fast Running. He ran between the two elm trees, racing as fast as he could, faster than the wind.

"Little Red Squirrel," his daddy called after him.
"Did I tell you today that I love you?"

"Because why?" asked Little Red Squirrel. (He was spinning now, faster and faster, round and round in circles.)

"Daddy," said the spinning Little Red Squirrel. "Do you love me because I'm fast?" (Then he fell over, of course, because he was so dizzy.)

"No," his daddy laughed, picking him up.

"That's not why."

Next Little Red Squirrel showed his dad his Undercover
Stash of Top Secret Berries he'd been collecting.

They counted them together. There were A Lot. It took
A Long Time.

"Daddy?" asked Little Red Squirrel, bouncing up and down.

"Do you love me because I'm so good at finding all these berries?"

"You are VERY good at finding berries." His daddy smiled.
"But that's not why I love you."

Now Little Red Squirrel showed
his dad his High Climbing.

He scrambled up the great oak, all the way up,
straight to the top. His dad climbed after him.

"Daddy?" whispered Little Red Squirrel.
"Do you love me because I'm strong and can do such High Climbing?"
"No," his daddy said. "That's not why."

Now Little Red Squirrel showed his dad his Brave Balancing. He darted from branch to branch, leaping out into the wide-open air.

"Daddy!" cried Little Red Squirrel. "Maybe . . .
do you love me because I'm so ABSOLUTELY brave?"
"No," his daddy said, and winked. "That's not why."

Little Red Squirrel started
cleaning his shiny red coat.

Then he got an idea. "I know, Daddy!" he
cried, waving his fluffy tail. "You love me
because I'm so COMPLETELY handsome!"

"You are VERY handsome," said his daddy, laughing and
chasing Little Red Squirrel to the foot of the great oak.
"But that's not why I love you."

Little Red Squirrel was getting very sleepy now.
And it was way past his bedtime.

As they walked home, Little Red Squirrel yawned a big yawn and reached up so his daddy could carry him.

"Daddy," he said, looking into his daddy's eyes.
"Maybe . . . do you love me because I'm Friendly?"

"No," the daddy laughed. And kissed his nose.
"That's not why I love you."

The daddy gently tucked his little squirrel into his cozy nest.

"Little Red Squirrel, you are very fast, and smart, and handsome, and friendly, and good at finding berries . . .

"And you are very strong and brave . . .

"But that's not why I love you."

And his daddy kissed the top of his little squirrel head.

And took his little squirrel hand. And whispered into his little squirrel ear . . .

"No, little one," he said . . .

"I love you just because you're mine."